Bill the Warthog MYSTERIES

BOX OFFICE Bill

An imprint of Rose Publishing, Inc.
Carson, CA
www.Rose-Publishing.com

Read more about your favorite tusked detective in these Bill the Warthog Mysteries:

Bill the Warthog MYSTERIES

BOX OFFICE Bill

Dean A. Anderson

For my brothers and sisters:
Gwynne, Daryl, Lola and Dale.
Thanks for living out the Beatitudes for me
to follow in your paths.

BILL THE WARTHOG MYSTERIES: BOX OFFICE BILL
©2014 by Dean Anderson
ISBN 10: 1-58411-141-0
ISBN 13: 978-1-58411-141-2
RoseKidz® #L48308
JUVENILE FICTION / Religious / Christian / General

RoseKidz®
An imprint of Rose Publishing, Inc.
17909 Adria Maru Lane
Carson, CA 90746
www.Rose-Publishing.com

Cover and interior illustrator: Aburtov and Graphikslava

Printed in South Korea   *03 0416 APC*

Table of Contents

Chapter 1

The Case of
the Rival Detective

43! This was the tallest tower ever, so obviously I was nervous. One false movement would send everything crashing to the ground and I don't have to say what a mess that would make.

Then Bill did something that spelled disaster. There was a knock at the door and Bill slammed the book he was reading on his desk. The 43 potato chips that I had stacked carefully in what probably was a record-making tower came crashing to the ground. (I read about a world record set by a guy who stacked 102 potato chips. But that person probably stacked with his hands, and I use my toes.)

"I hope it's a case," Bill said. I hoped for the same. Bill, as you may or may not know, is the world's only warthog

detective. But at the moment he had no case.

This is why on a muggy summer day, I resorted to seeing how many chips I could stack one on top of another and Bill was rereading one of his favorite *Father Brown* mysteries.

I opened the door and couldn't believe who I saw. It was a kid about my age. Adam Lee Balmer. Yeah, I know I don't need to tell you who he is. But I needed to tell Bill, once I was able to talk.

"Hi, my name is Adam. Is this the office of Bill the Warthog?"

"Um, yeah. I know who you are. My name is…um…"

"Aren't you Nick Sayga?" Adam asked.

"Yeah, you're right!" I said. "How'd you know?"

"I've read all your books," Adam said. "Hey, there's the man, I mean, the warthog himself! Great to see you, Bill!"

"I'm sorry," Bill said. "Have we met before?"

"Bill! This is Adam Lee Balmer! You know, he plays Bumpknot, kid sidekick to Captain Galactus on *Space Stuff*, the greatest science fiction show ever!"

(I had never really watched *Space Stuff* until we had a case involving the show. I then asked for a DVD set of the first season for Christmas and have loved it ever since.)

The next few moments were amazing, as Adam raved on and on about what a fan he was of Bill's. Then I said what a fan I was of Adam's.

"You know," he said, "I have to admit I doubted that you were really an actual warthog. But here you are with the tusks and hooves and warts!"

"I appreciate your kind words," Bill said. "What can I do for you?"

"Oh, right," Adam said. "I'm sorry. I know your time is valuable."

"Yeah, valuable time," I thought. *"Bill's reading that book for the tenth time."*

"I'm in your town filming a new movie. I was wondering if you could come by the set and give us some tips," Adam said.

"Is it a film about warthogs?" Bill asked.

"No," Adam said. "I'm sorry, I can't tell you much now. The producers are keeping security tight. There's a rumor another studio is trying to steal some of our ideas. Just come to this address tomorrow morning at 8:00."

Adam gave Bill a card with an address.

The next morning at 8:00 sharp, we were at that address, an old warehouse.

At the gate was a tall man in a trench coat and fedora

hat, not unlike the coat and hat Bill usually wears.

"Do you have a pass?" the man said.

"I have this card with the address," Bill said.

"Adam Lee Balmer himself invited us," I said.

"Yeah, and the Man in the Moon asked me over for pizza. Scram kid, and whatever you are."

"I'm a warthog," Bill said, "and I assume you're providing security of some sort? May I ask your name?"

"Yeah, I'm providing security here. My name is Milo Bowman. I'm a private detective."

"Should we come back later?" I asked Bill.

"You're giving up too early, kid," Milo said. "I might let you through, if you happen to drop some scratch in my palm."

"You want me attack your hand?" I asked.

"I think he means," Bill said, "if we give him money, he'll let us in."

"Your hairy friend here ain't all stupid," Milo said.

I saw Adam behind Milo's back.

"Hey, Adam," I called out.

"Nick! Bill!" Adam shouted. "These are the guys I was telling you about," he said to a tall man wearing a baseball cap.

Adam was dressed in shorts, T-shirt and tennis shoes. I had kind of hoped he would be wearing his space uniform

from *Space Stuff.* He introduced us to the man with the baseball cap.

"This is the director of this film, Cameron Gore."

"I see you already met our director of security, Milo Bowman," Mr. Gore said.

"Yes," Bill said, "and I'd like to talk to you about that."

Milo looked worried. "Don't listen to what this creature has to say. He and his friend tried to bribe me into letting them in the studio."

"Oh really," Bill said. "Tell us more."

"This creature and the kid each tried to hand me a bill. But I wasn't about to let them both in for a lousy $50."

"So how high does the bribe have to be, Mr. Bowman?" Bill asked. "Mr. Gore, I thought Adam might have asked us here to help with security. It looks like that may still be a need here, from what I've seen."

"Hey," Milo said, "I'm the best there is."

"Actually," Mr. Gore said, "Adam suggested you come to consult on our script. It's about a wombat detective. Adam thought you might be able to give us some insight into what it's like to be a strange mammal detective in a human world."

"Nick and I would be happy to help, but can I tell you something about Mr. Bowman here?"

Mr. Gore nodded and Bill whispered in his ear.

"You're right, Mr. Warthog," Mr. Gore said. "Unfortunately, I can't fire Mr. Bowman—he's a professional, licensed detective hired by the studio. But would you be willing to work here and provide a second eye for security?"

"Certainly," Bill said. "I'm glad to see you saw the fault in Mr. Bowman's accusation. I like your attitude of not taking things at their face value. You might say I like the way you understand the Beatitudes."

Adam turned to me. *"What did Milo say wrong? And what are Beatitudes?"*

☞ **Turn to page 92 to find out!**

Chapter 2

The Case of Seeing Double

43! This was the tallest tower ever, so obviously I was nervous. One false movement would send everything crashing to the ground and I don't have to say what a mess that would make.

I know, some of you are thinking, *I've already read this chapter.* But Bill and I were back at his office and I was trying to see if I could get the chip pile any higher. But I couldn't.

Bill was reading again, but this time it was books about movie making. He was trying to learn as much as he could before we went back over to work at the studio.

(Have I ever told you that Bill still prefers to look up things in books rather than online? He says his hooves work fine turning

pages, but they do have trouble with computer keyboards.)

Anyway, there was a knock on the door, again. I opened the door and said, "Adam!"

The kid at the door said, "Huh?"

I'm sure Bill saw that we both were pretty confused.

"Oh, you're not Adam," I said. It was a kid Adam's age and height and coloring. But it wasn't Adam. He looked a lot like him, though.

"I'm Rudy Myer," the kid said holding out his hand to shake. "Is this the Warthog Detective Agency?"

"It is," I said, "But if you have a case, we're going to be kind of busy these days. My name's Nick."

"I'm not here with a case, I was wondering if you might need help. I'm looking for a job and I heard that this place hired kids," Rudy said.

"I don't know where you heard that, but I'm the only kid who works here and not for money. Bill and I are friends," I said.

Bill came to the door and Rudy looked surprised, as people often do when they first see Bill. But he then told Bill his story.

Rudy's dad had lost his job a few months ago and was looking for work. His mom had a job, but it was just part time. Rudy wanted to help the family out, so he decided to

see if he could get a summer job.

"There aren't many jobs for children," Bill said, "and for good reason. Usually kids should be in school. But I have an idea for a summer job for you."

Rudy went with Bill and me to the movie set. We watched Bill talk to Mr. Gore. The director kept looking over at Rudy and nodding and smiling. Finally, they walked over.

"You're right, Bill, this young man would make an ideal double for Adam. Let me call him over," Mr. Gore said.

Adam stood next to Rudy and they did look like long lost cousins.

Rudy then asked the question that I'd been wanting to ask, "What exactly is a double?"

Bill said, "Sometimes, in movies and TV they hire someone who looks like an actor to stand in while they're setting up the lights and cameras. Sometimes a double will even fill in if an actor can't make it to film a long shot or a shot from behind."

"It can be a little dull," Mr. Gore said. "But the money isn't bad."

"That would be great," Rudy said.

"We will have to talk to your parents and you'll need to fill out these papers. You'll find the copy machine in that office.

Make three copies and get it all filled out by tomorrow."

I walked with Rudy to the office while Bill stayed behind to talk to the director. I thought I was seeing double for the second time that day. I saw someone, or something, wearing a trench coat and a fedora hat just like Bill's. And the face was furry.

I was thinking I better have my mom make me an eye doctor's appointment.

We went in the office and found the copy machine. While Rudy made his copies, I took a look around the office.

On a desk was a script. The title on the cover got my attention: *Arnie the Wombat Detective*. I was beginning to understand why Adam had contacted Bill. I was going to have to ask about this.

When Rudy was finished with his copies, I had one of my not-so-good ideas: "Rudy, why don't we have fun with the copy machine?"

"I don't think that's a good idea," he said.

But I made copies of my face, hands, and, of course, my toes. Rudy did not join in.

Then Adam invited us into the trailer so he could get to know Rudy. It was a pretty cool little place with a fridge, bed and video game system.

But before we could get the glasses of water that Adam offered, there was a knock at the door.

Outside we saw Bill, Mr. Gore and Milo looking very serious.

"I'm telling you, Mr. Gore," Milo said, "you need to let me check people out before you let them on the set. Especially some poor kid like this who would probably do anything for money."

"What is this all about?" Adam asked.

"Mr. Bowman here is making a rather serious charge," Mr. Gore said. "He thinks Rudy was copying pages from this script that someone foolishly left in the office and was planning on selling them to another studio or a movie website."

Mr. Gore was holding the script I had seen in the office.

"He might have gotten away with it," Milo said, "but I checked the paper counter on the copy machine and there were more copies made than Rudy would need for the paper work."

I felt pretty bad at that moment. "I can explain the extra copies," I said.

I pulled the copies I'd made of my face out of my pockets and told them. Mr. Gore and Adam laughed when they saw the pictures. Milo didn't laugh and neither did Bill.

Mr. Gore said he was going to hire Rudy if his parents approved. Bill told me I should pay ten cents a copy and clean off the glass on the machine. So I did.

"Later I talked to Bill. I asked him if Rudy wouldn't have been hired if I hadn't confessed.

"No," Bill said. "I could have proven you made the extra copies, Nick, if it came to that. But I have to hand it to you; you really put your foot in it this time. I was more concerned with the way Milo Bowman marked Rudy out, just because he's poor. That's not the right beatitude to have about people."

How could Bill have shown Rudy hadn't made the copies of the script on the machine?

And what is the right attitude (or beatitude) to have about the poor?

 **Turn to page 94 to find out!**

Chapter 3

The Case of the Purple Tears

I admit I spend too much time looking up funny or cool things on the Internet. Sometimes I share with Bill the things I find, like exploding soda bottles or squirrels playing with an elephant at the zoo.

This video I found online was not funny or cool.

It was video taken on Adam's movie set showing a very phony looking wombat mask on an actor wearing a fedora and a trench coat.

On the website were a whole bunch of comments on how corny the costume looked and, therefore, how bad the movie was going to be.

I called Bill, who said he was about to call me because

the director, Mr. Gore, had called *him*.

I took my bike and met Bill at the set. Mr. Gore and Milo, the detective, were waiting for us.

"Bill, I'm so glad to see you," Mr. Gore said. "I assume you've seen the pictures on the Internet."

"Mr. Gore," Milo said, "I have everything under control."

"If that's so, I'd hate to see what you consider chaos, Milo," Gore responded. "Bill, let me update you on the situation."

The director explained some things we'd only guessed at before. The movie they were making was about a wombat detective and his human friend. The human friend was the role that Adam was playing. It was becoming very clear why Adam had come to us for advice.

They weren't using a real wombat to play the detective. They were using a human actor with a cheesy mask. But they were planning on using computer-generated imagery ("CGI, as they call it in the movie biz," Bill later told me) to replace the mask.

The pictures on the Internet made the whole film look cheesy, but the wombat in the film would not look like that at all.

Mr. Gore said they had tracked down the computer the images had been posted from. It was in a public library next

door to the set.

"So we need to find out who's putting these unauthorized photos and videos on the web," Mr. Gore said.

"Who could have taken pictures of the actor in the wombat mask?" Bill asked.

"Just about anybody on the set," Milo said. "There were dozens of people with access, including you and your little friend here."

Just then, Adam came running toward us. "More pictures have been posted," he said, "of me."

Adam showed us pictures on his cell phone. They were pictures of Adam crying. There was a caption on the pictures that read, "Adam Lee Balmer in tears because of how horribly his new film is turning out!"

"Gee, Adam, are you really that upset about how the film is turning out?" I asked.

"No, Nick, these pictures were taken when I was filming a scene for the film. In the scene I've been told the Wombat Detective is dead."

"The good news is this really narrows down who posted these pictures, Mr. Gore said. "There were only three people on the set when that scene was filmed."

"Gather those three people together in your office, Mr. Gore," Bill said. "Let's see if we can get this little mystery solved."

"Hey," Milo said, "I was going to say that!"

"Too late," I said under my breath.

I went with Bill, Mr. Gore and Milo to an office where three people were already seated in plush chairs.

"Bill, this is our cameraman, James Wong," Mr. Gore said. "Our gaffer, Eddie Tomison, who does the lighting. And Ron Pipes, one of our make-up people."

"All right," Milo said sternly. "I want to know what you saw and when you saw it."

"I'm sorry," said Mr. Wong. "The only thing I saw was what I saw through the lens of this camera."

"That's true," Mr. Gore said. "I don't see when Jimmy would have had his eye off the camera. But come to think of it, I did see Eddie and Ron with their cell phones that day."

"So either of them could have taken pictures of Adam crying in this scene," Milo said. "Speak up and tell us who did this, or you'll both find yourselves out on the street."

"I'm sorry, I didn't see anything," Ron said. "I'd help if I could."

Eddie sat there for a moment, then he pulled out a

handkerchief and rubbed his eyes. I could see his eyes were all teary. "Okay, I didn't want to say anything. But I saw Ron take the pictures. Sorry, Ron, but I have to tell the truth."

"What? I didn't. I might have made a phone call but that's all I used my phone for that day."

"Do you have any questions, Bill?" Mr. Gore asked.

Bill went over to Ron and sniffed the air. Then he went by Eddie and sniffed the air.

"Something doesn't smell right. So, why do you think you're crying, Eddie?" Bill asked.

"I'm just so sad about Ron; having to tell you that he took those pictures of Adam crying and the wombat mask. He'll probably lose his job now."

"I have another question, Eddie," Bill said. "What have you been eating?"

"What does that have to do with anything?" Eddie said. "I've had a donut, some coffee. Why?"

"Just wondering," Bill said. "Say there's something on your cheek. Nick, can you see what that is?"

The thing on Eddie's cheek seemed like a small piece of skin. But it was purple.

"That's some great detective work," Milo said. "Aren't you going to ask Ron what he had for lunch? I had grilled cheese,

if it matters. Let's just get this make-up guy off the lot."

"Why do you believe Eddie's story, Milo?" Bill asked.

"Because of the tears," Milo said.

"That's why I don't believe him," Bill said. "Though real tears are the beginning of blessing, they can be a sign of the right beatitude. I hope you'll learn that, Eddie."

Why didn't Bill believe Eddie's tears? Why did Bill say that tears can be the beginning of blessing?

 **Turn to page 96 to find out!**

Chapter 4

The Case of the Temporary Diamonds

"This is very silly," Bill said. "Whoever heard of such a thing? A wombat detective? I don't think so."

"It's not meant to be real," I said to Bill. "It's just a movie. Give it a chance and read some more."

Bill and I had been asked to read the script of the film. It was called *Arnie the Wombat Detective,* but Mr. Gore said that was the working title and it could change.

We weren't supposed to take the script off set, so they had set up one of the trailers as a reading room. It was very cool.

There were no video games, like in Adam's trailer, but there were big, comfy chairs. It had a fridge stocked full of fruit juice and milk. I was hoping that it would be stocked with soda, but they must have checked with my mom. At least there was chocolate milk.

They had given scripts to Bill and me and we were stretched out in our comfy chairs to read for the afternoon.

Anyway, I convinced Bill to read some more and he started to get into it. I checked with the studio to see if I could use a part of the script in this book and they said it was okay.

A script is set up different from a regular book. A lot of it is dialogue, people (or a wombat) talking and then paragraphs in a different type that describe the setting and actions.

So here is a section of *Arnie the Wombat Detective*. After you read this, I'll tell you what Bill said about it.

• •

SCENE 24

(THE SETTING IS THE SECURITY OFFICE OF THE LUKE MATTHEWS DIAMOND COMPANY. ONE WALL IS COVERED WITH TELEVISION MONITORS. OPPOSITE THE MONITORS ARE TALL, SOLIDLY LOCKED METAL DOORS.

ARNIE THE WOMBAT DETECTIVE AND HIS FRIEND SCOOTER ARE IN CONVERSATION WITH STUD KNUCKLEBREATH, HEAD OF SECURITY, AND RODNEY WEALTHYPANTS, THE COMPANY PRESIDENT)

STUD: The cameras captured the whole thing. But they didn't capture the robbery.

SCOOTER: But that doesn't make any sense at all.

ARNIE: So, you are saying the cameras filmed the robbery of the diamonds…but they didn't film the robbery of the diamonds?

STUD: Exactly.

RODNEY: Only twenty diamonds were taken of the thousands we own. But these were the twenty most valuable diamonds worth millions of dollars. Perhaps it would be best if you show the film footage, Stud.

(THE CAMERA FOCUSES ON ONE OF THE TELEVISION MONITORS, WHERE WE SEE A DISPLAY CASE WITH TWENTY LARGE DIAMONDS. A FIGURE IN A BLACK CAP COMES BETWEEN THE CAMERA AND THE DISPLAY CASE. HE IS HOLDING A VELVET BAG.

AFTER SEVERAL MOMENTS, THE FIGURE TURNS TO THE CAMERA SHOWING HIS FACE. IT IS A UNIQUE FACE, TATTOOED WITH ORANGE AND WHITE STRIPES. HE SMILES, THEN LEAVES THE ROOM.

IT APPEARS ALL THE DIAMONDS ARE STILL IN THE DISPLAY CASE.)

STUD: And here is the same display case now.

(THE TELEVISION MONITOR SHOWS AN EMPTY DISPLAY CASE.)

SCOOTER: Holy missing diamonds, Arnie, how can that be?

ARNIE: Am I correct in assuming the cameras are motion activated?

STUD: That's right. They turn on when there is movement in the room. They activated when that strange man entered the room. And the cameras shut off when he left the room with the diamonds still intact.

RODNEY: And the cameras should have activated if anyone else entered the room, but there's nothing.

SCOOTER: We know that man. He's Arnie's archenemy, Anthony "The Tiger" Caton. The fiend!

RODNEY: But the footage won't convict this Tiger fellow of the crime. Perhaps we can get the police to arrest him for breaking and entering because he should not have been in that room.

STUD: But the cameras show the diamonds there after the robbery. So who took them?

ARNIE: I think I know. But tell me, Stud, did you find any water on the floor beneath the display case?

STUD: Yes, how did you know?

ARNIE: Just an educated guess. I think Scooter and I will pay a visit to Mr. Caton.

(CUT TO ARNIE AND SCOOTER AT THE FRONT DOOR OF A LARGE MANSION. SCOOTER RINGS THE DOORBELL. "THE TIGER" HIMSELF ANSWERS THE DOOR. HE IS STILL WEARING THE BLACK CAP AND HIS FACE STILL HAS THE ORANGE AND WHITE STRIPES)

THE TIGER: I wondered how long it would take for you to come, Mr. Wombat. I see you brought your stupid little friend.

ARNIE: Insults are beneath you, Tiger.

THE TIGER: Everything is beneath me, the greatest criminal genius of all time.

ARNIE: You do have a rather high opinion of yourself, don't you, Tiger?

THE TIGER: Why shouldn't I, Wombat? No one can imagine how I do the things I do, let alone pull them off.

ARNIE: Oh, I may have an idea how you did what you did. I've been doing a little research on diamonds. Would you like to know what I've learned?

THE TIGER: Oh, certainly. I'm sure this will be fascinating.

ARNIE: Diamonds are the only gems composed of

one element, carbon. They are formed when great pressure and heat come together far beneath the earth's surface. The circumstances must be just right, which is what makes them so valuable.

THE TIGER: Yes, diamonds are pricey rocks. I know that. I know everything.

ARNIE: Here's another interesting fact: diamonds sometimes go by the nickname of "ice."

THE TIGER: Perhaps you know a little more than I thought you did. I think our visit is done here, and you should go closer to where diamonds are made.

(THE TIGER PULLS A LEVER AND A TRAPDOOR OPENS UNDER ARNIE AND SCOOTER. THEY FALL INTO AN UNDERGROUND DUNGEON WHERE THEY ARE SURROUNDED BY REAL TIGERS.)

• •

I wasn't expecting that tiger pit. I'm sure the movie audiences won't be expecting it either. I asked Bill what he thought of the script.

"Well, like so many Hollywood films, it doesn't sound like realism is too high a priority. I mean a wombat detective, really?"

"But could you figure out the mystery, Bill? How did that Tiger guy steal the diamonds?"

"That's simple, Nick. That Tiger fellow thinks too much of himself. He should learn to be meek, then he could get a lot more than just diamonds. He could get the whole earth, in fact."

Can you figure out how the diamonds were taken? And what is Bill talking about? What is it to be "meek" and what do you get out of such a thing?

☞ **Turn to page 98 to find out!**

Chapter 5

The Case of
the Peanut Dust

We got to the set a little late the next day and we were surprised to see that everyone else seemed to be leaving. Rudy was just heading out the gate, so we stopped him and asked him what was going on.

"All the filming today was supposed to feature Adam, and he couldn't do anything today, so they told most of us to go home," Rudy said.

"What's wrong with Adam," I asked. "Is he sick? Is he hurt?"

"You can see him for yourself," Rudy said. "He's in his trailer."

Bill knocked on the door of Adam's trailer, and Adam

invited us in. Adam's face looked pretty awful, even a little scary.

His face was all swollen up. Once at our school we had a contest to see who could stuff the most marshmallows into his mouth without swallowing. Martin Stevens managed 23. But Adam's face looked like he'd stuffed in 50 or so.

"Wow," I said. "Is that make-up? If so, Mr. Pipes did pretty amazing work!"

"No, Nick," Adam said, "it's not make-up. It's an allergic reaction. We think it's from something I ate that the catering company sent over. The doctor said I should be okay by tomorrow."

(I should say something here about that catering company, Foodz R Uz. They were amazing. They supplied breakfast, lunch and dinner on the set — and snacks too. The food was all very tasty but it was really healthy. And they made special orders. When Bill started working on the set they made him a special centipede soup. No, you don't want to see what it looked or smelled like.)

"So, do you know what caused the allergic reaction?" Bill asked.

"I'm allergic to peanuts," Adam said.

"But don't the caterers know about your allergy? I would

think they would try to be careful about such a thing," Bill said.

"Oh, they know," Adam said. "They've been contacted about the dietary needs of everyone who works here. Why else would they have maggot pita sandwiches served to you, Bill?"

"True," Bill said. "What did you eat today, Adam?"

"I had a cheese omelet."

"Could someone have snuck peanuts into it without your noticing it?" Bill asked.

"I had some pretty hot salsa on top of the omelet, so yeah, it's possible," Adam said.

There was a knock on the door. I opened the door to see Milo Bowman. "You can go home, Warthog," he said. "I've got this one solved."

"Oh, really?" Bill said.

"Yeah, it's obviously the kid who brought the food to Adam in the trailer; he's waiting in the security office for the police to pick him up. He's got some crazy story about being stopped by a giant squirrel."

"Let's talk to this guy," Bill said to me.

I knew the kid in the security office, Massimo Tuscany. I'd seen him bringing food to the production team since I'd started coming to the set.

"Massimo," I said, "I can't believe you would do this to Adam. What happened?"

"Thanks for coming to see me, Nick and Bill. I'm not sure what happened. I was bringing Adam his omelet, and I was stopped by a guy in a squirrel costume. He said he had a part in the movie."

"Did he ask you to do anything for him?" Bill asked.

"Yes," Massimo said. "He asked me to zip up the back of his suit."

"Did you set down Adam's tray?" Bill asked.

"Yeah, I did."

"Did the squirrel get between you and the tray?" Bill asked.

"Come to think of it, he did."

"So is it possible," Bill asked, "that the squirrel put something in the salsa or the omelet while you were zipping the back of the costume?"

"You're right! I bet that's what happened!"

We left the office, and I asked Bill what we should do next.

Bill said, "There's just one place I know to look for a giant squirrel."

We went several blocks to the Nutty Costume Shop. And there we found a guy in a squirrel costume. Actually, we saw a squirrel body with a human head. He was holding

the squirrel head under his arm. He had a giant acorn under the other arm.

When we approached him, he looked nervous. His tail swished. I saw on the Nutty sign that it was still five minutes until the store would open.

"Excuse me, sir," Bill said. "Were you just at the movie set down the street?"

"Yeah, what's it to you?" the squirrel man said.

"It's a matter of security," Bill said. "May I ask your name?"

"Rodney," he said.

"And what were you doing at that set?"

"Well, I'm something of a squirrel expert, and I was hoping they might find a part for me in the movie, since I heard they had talking animals."

"Oh, really?" Bill said. "You do know that the movie is about a wombat detective, and wombats are from Australia?"

"Of course," Rodney said. "I was going to play an Australian squirrel. I would be awesome in this."

"Nick, could you look inside that giant acorn of his?"

Rodney took off in a sprint. At least as much of a sprint as you can make in a squirrel costume. I took off after him.

I dived for his tail and caught it. Rodney fell face first on the ground. The acorn went flying.

Bill sat on Rodney and held him down while I fetched the acorn. The top had come off of it and brown dust spread on the ground. I put a finger in the dust and sniffed it.

The dust was ground up peanut.

The police came and picked up Rodney. They took the squirrel costume as evidence.

"So Bill, why didn't you believe Rodney?" I asked.

"You'd have to be nuts to think he was a squirrel expert," Bill said. "But just as squirrels hunger for nuts, Rodney better start hungering for what's right."

How did Bill know Rodney was not telling the truth? And what's this about hungering for what's right?

👉 **Turn to page 100 to find out!**

Chapter 6

The Case of the Sloppy Stunt

I was hanging onto the riggings for lights 40 feet above the ground and thinking, "I hope I don't fall." I was also thinking, "I hope my mom doesn't hear about this."

But you'd probably like to know how I got there.

Adam had told us that they were going to be filming some of the stunts for the climax of the movie, and I was excited.

We arrived at the set early and found two new people standing at the gate. Milo Bowman came to meet them.

"I'm Ralph from the ACME Stunt Company," said a man wearing a solid green shirt and blue jeans.

"I'm Sam from the ACME Stunt Company," said the

other man, wearing a solid red shirt and black jeans. "I thought I was the only one sent for this job."

"I thought I was the only one sent to do this job," Ralph said.

"Why don't you both come in," Milo said, "and we'll straighten this out later."

"I have a bad feeling about this," Bill said to me. "I had better talk to Mr. Gore." Bill went in Mr. Gore's office with Milo.

Adam had told me about the scene they were going to film that day. Adam's character was going to confront a henchman for Arnie the Wombat's archenemy, The Tiger, on top of Luke Matthews Diamond Company.

The crew had set up to film the scene by setting up riggings that would double as the building. They had a green screen set up behind the rigging so a computer could impose images of the building in its place.

While I waited, I saw Sam climb up and inspect the riggings. After he climbed down, I saw Ralph climb up.

I went to Adam's trailer to see if he wanted to play video games. But Adam wasn't there, and the trailer was locked.

I went back to the set where they were going to film the stunt. No one was around.

I thought it would be fun to climb up and look at the place they were going to film. My worst idea since I decided to play with the copy machine. No, it was worse than that idea.

There was a rope ladder to climb up to the riggings. When I was about halfway up, I thought, "Hey, this isn't  so high!" When I got to the top, I thought, "Hey, I was wrong when I thought this isn't so high!"

There was a narrow platform at the top. I climbed up on the platform. There was a loud creaking sound.

I kept walking anyway. The creaking got louder.

Then the creaking stopped because the platform gave way. Fortunately, I'd been holding on to the riggings for the lighting as I told you when you first learned my life was in danger.

I yelled very loud. "Help! Someone, help!"

"Hold on tight!" Bill yelled to me. "Quick, someone get me the safety harness!"

(How was I supposed to know there was a safety harness?)

I was amazed at how quickly Bill climbed that ladder. He brought a rope up in his mouth. When he got to the top, he threw the rope over one of the rafters, tied it around my chest, and I was lowered to the ground.

I still have no idea how he did all this, considering he has hooves rather than hands.

Bill was still at the top of the rope ladder. "Someone sabotaged the platform," he called to us. "Someone removed the bolts at the end of the platform."

"I saw Ralph and Sam up there while you were all in the office," I said.

"So," Milo said, "which one of you supposed stunt men did this?"

"It wasn't me," Sam said. "I was planning on filming that scene today. Would I have risked my own life?"

"Don't look at me," Ralph said. "I was planning on being up there for that scene today."

"Who's telling the truth?" Mr. Gore asked.

"I think I know," Bill said as he jumped from the ladder to the floor. "But I need to ask a question of whoever is in charge of costumes."

Mr. Gore called for Ethel Noggin, the wardrobe coordinator. Bill whispered a question in her ear.

"No, I didn't think I'd have to provide a shirt for the stunt man for the scene," Ms. Noggin said.

"Someone could have been badly hurt, even killed," Bill said. "Mr. Miles, please call the police and ask them to arrest Ralph."

"Why do you think I did it?" Ralph asked. Bill didn't tell him, but he did tell the police when they came.

Sam and some of the crew members fixed the platform and checked and rechecked it. Then we watched the scene filmed.

In the scene, Sam played Joe Egypt, one of The Tiger's henchmen. Joe tries to push Adam's character off the platform, but stumbles.

Sam was in the same place I'd been early in the day, hanging by his fingers forty feet above the ground. (Except he was wearing the safety harness.)

In the scene, Adam's character pulls Joe to safety.

On the way home, I said to Bill, "I know it's just a movie, but…"

"But what?" Bill asked.

"If I was Adam's character in the movie and someone tried to push me…"

"Yes?" Bill said.

"I'm not sure I'd help them back up. I might let them fall," I said.

"You're still shook up from the accident this morning," Bill said.

"Maybe so."

"It's important to show mercy if you want mercy," Bill said.

"Why do I need mercy?" I asked.

"We all need mercy," Bill said, "according to the Beatitudes."

"The Beatitudes again?" I said. "Say, could you tell me how you knew Ralph was the one who had sabotaged the platform?"

Why did Bill suspect Ralph of sabotaging the platform? What do the Beatitudes have to say about mercy?

 **Turn to page 102 to find out!**

Chapter 7

The Case
of the Z Word

So, at first I wasn't sure how I was going to write this chapter. You see, my mom reads these books and I didn't see how I'd write this without getting into trouble. Because to tell what happened, I thought I was going to have to use a certain word.

It's an important part of the story, so I thought I had to use it somehow. I thought about doing what they do sometimes in the newspaper, type the word but leave out a couple of letters. But then some kids would probably try to figure out which letters to fill in and that wouldn't be good.

But I won't keep you waiting about how this all happened. Adam came over to my house one night. It was exciting to introduce a movie star to my parents, but they pretty much just treated him like one of my friends.

We went to my room and mom brought us lemonade and cookies.

When my mom left the room, Adam said, "I don't know what to do, Nick. The writers added something to the script. They want me to say the Z word."

I was pretty shocked. And you would have been too if I had put in the word that Adam meant.

"Why?" I asked. "Don't they know kids will be coming to this movie? Especially with you in it."

"Yeah, but the producers are afraid teens might not come if the movie is rated 'G,' so they want me to say the word to get a harsher rating," Adam said. "They say older kids won't go to a 'G' film."

"Can you tell them you won't do it?" I asked.

"I guess. I don't know. I'm used to just doing what the director tells me," he said.

I thought we would end up hearing more about that word on the set the next day, but we were confronted with it sooner than I expected.

All along the warehouse that housed the set for the film, someone had spray-painted in large, black letters the

word "ZARP."

Inside, we saw the director, Mr. Gore, and Bill said, "I noticed the graffiti outside. Do you want me to investigate the matter?"

"Actually, Bill, it's already been dealt with," Mr. Gore said. "Milo and his new assistant tracked down the guilty parties. He's with them in my office waiting for the police to pick them up."

We went with Mr. Gore into the office. Milo Bowman was standing there along with two kids sitting in chairs. The kids sitting in the chairs had clothes speckled with black paint.

"Hey Warthog, I actually followed your example in something," Milo said. "I decided to get an assistant. Meet Marvin Brown."

The kid who was standing nodded his head. I recognized him as part of Chris Franklin's gang from Chris' more troublesome days.

"Marvin was going to meet me here early," Milo said, "And he heard something in the bushes, so he gave chase."

"I yelled, 'Hey,'" Marvin said, continuing the story. "I ran toward the sound and I came around the building and found these two punks standing there with a spray paint can on the ground between them.

"And so I said to them…"

Okay, I'm not going to quote Marvin exactly here because he used a lot of words, including "zarp," but also other words I won't write. (Including one that I didn't know. Bill assured me it wasn't worth learning.)

Basically what he said was, "Hey, you [bad words], don't deny you did this zarp. Stay right here or I'll [bad words] beat you up."

"So, I grabbed them both by their collars," Marvin said, "And brought them inside."

One of the kids was named Ian and he said, "I didn't do it! I was just standing around, hoping to get Adam Balmer to sign my autograph book. This kid came around the corner and sprayed me with the paint can, then dropped it between us."

The other kid named Shane said, "*I* was the one standing around hoping for an autograph when *he* sprayed me with paint and dropped the can."

"I think they're both lying," Milo said, "so I called the police and they can take them both in."

"First of all," Bill said, "congratulations Milo and Marvin on catching at least one of the trouble makers. Is there an autograph book?"

Marvin brought it out. "Is there a name on it?" Bill asked.

"The name on the cover got covered with spray paint," Marvin said.

"All right," said Bill. "We might still be able to figure out who this autograph book belongs to. Ian, Shane, please empty your pockets."

Ian and Shane emptied their pockets. When we saw something that had been in Ian's pocket, but not in Shane's, we knew that Ian was the one probably telling us the truth.

The police came and talked to Ian and Shane and took Shane downtown and said they would call his parents. Ian was able to get autographs from just about everyone on the set, including from Bill and me, before he left.

Mr. Gore said to Bill. "Well, that was upsetting and a waste of time."

"Yes," Bill said, "I was bothered by the word on the wall and even some of the things Marvin said. Where do kids get the idea that using language like that is okay?"

Mr. Gore was very quiet. But soon he called Adam to his office.

Adam came to Bill and me and said, "Great news! Mr. Gore cut that word from my script!"

"That's good," Bill said. "What we say is important because it can show what is in our hearts. And if our hearts are pure, we'll get to see something much better than any of your TV shows or movies, Adam. No offense."

What did Ian have in his pocket that showed he was more likely the innocent party? What is Bill talking about when he said that people who are pure in heart will see something great?

☞ **Turn to page 104 to find out!**

Chapter 8

The Case of Fighting Like Cats and Dogs

I don't get a lot of the mail at my house, so I was surprised when my mom said there was a special delivery and I needed to sign for it.

I was excited to see that the package came from Adam Lee Balmer. Adam and the rest of the crew from the film had finished filming the week before and had gone back to Hollywood to complete editing and special effects.

I opened it to find a script and a short note from Adam. The note read:

Hey Nick,

It was great to meet you and Bill and work with you this summer. I'm sending you this rewrite of the script. There are some interesting changes and I'd like you to look it over and let me know what you think.

Hope you and Bill can come out for the film's debut next year.

All the best,

Adam

It was about lunch time, so I went to the kitchen, made a peanut butter and jelly sandwich, cut up an apple, poured myself a glass of milk and took it along with my script to my room and started eating and reading.

Most of the script was the same, but there were some changes to the ending. So I skimmed the scenes that hadn't seemed to change.

I skipped over the part where Arnie the wombat detective and Scooter find that The Tiger and Rodney Wealthypants (president of the Luke Matthews Diamond Company) are actually the same person.

What seemed to have changed was the explanation of The Tiger's big plan. Instead of holding all of the world's diamonds for ransom, The Tiger was shown trying to start a war between two countries. He wanted to make a fortune by selling weapons to both sides.

Here are a couple of the new scenes in the script:

• •

(IN THE OFFICE OF ARNIE THE WOMBAT DETECTIVE)

SCOOTER: Somehow, Arnie, we've got to get into that meeting with The Tiger and the leaders of the nation of Felinia.

ARNIE: I've got a plan. The Tiger always serves pizza at his meetings. I've made an arrangement with the local pizza parlor so that when The Tiger calls out for pizza, we're delivering it.

(OUTSIDE THE DOOR OF THE FELINIA EMBASSY, SCOOTER AND ARNIE ARE IN PIZZA DELIVERY UNIFORMS)

ARNIE: Yuck, I can't stand the smell of these anchovy pizzas.

SCOOTER: You're one to talk, with your pizzas topped with tree bark.

ARNIE: Tree bark is very high in fiber.

SCOOTER: Let's go.

(AFTER KNOCKING ON THE DOOR, SCOOTER AND ARNIE ARE INVITED INTO THE ROOM. THEY FIND A LARGE TABLE SURROUNDED BY FELINIA OFFICIALS, INCLUDING THE AMBASSADOR. THE TIGER IS GIVING A POWERPOINT PRESENTATION.

PEOPLE FROM FELINIA ARE EASY TO SPOT

BECAUSE THEY ALWAYS DRESS IN RED.)

THE TIGER: I have evidence that the nation of Muttoria is planning to attack your nation. Your only chance is to attack them first. And I can sell you the weapons that will protect you.

AMBASSADOR: You keep on talking about this attack. But what is the nature of the attack?

THE TIGER: I'm glad you asked. As you know, the nation of Muttoria has more dogs than any nation in the world.

AMBASSADOR: Well, yes, everyone knows that the citizens of Muttoria love their puppies.

THE TIGER: We also all know that the people of Felinia always dress in red clothes.

AMBASSADOR: Well, of course, red is such a wonderful color and we all look splendid in red clothes. But what does any of this have to do with a Muttoria plot against Felinia?

THE TIGER: I'm getting there. I happen to know that the people of Muttoria are training their dogs to attack anyone who is wearing the color red. I believe they will send thousands and thousands of dogs into Felinia, and they will attack everyone wearing red clothes.

AMBASSADOR: You mean…

THE TIGER: Yes, dogs trained to attack people wearing

red would attack everyone in Felinia.

AMBASSADOR: That's horrible. What can we do to protect ourselves?

THE TIGER: The only way to protect yourselves is to attack Muttoria first. And I can sell you the weapons to do that.

(THE TIGER'S AIDE, STUD KNUCKLEBREATH, WHISPERS IN THE TIGER'S EAR.)

THE TIGER: Ambassador, I'm sorry to tell you there is a spy in the room. Possibly a spy from Muttoria. Those are not real pizza deliverers!

AMBASSADOR: Is this true? If so, you both will be arrested!

ARNIE: Mr. Ambassador, it is true I am not ordinarily a pizza deliverer, but you can see I am one today, since I delivered pizzas.

AMBASSADOR: Do you work for Muttoria?

ARNIE: I do not. But I do know you have no reason to go to war against them.

AMBASSADOR: But they're training their dogs to attack everyone who wears red. Of course we have to protect ourselves.

ARNIE: That isn't true. And if I could have a moment of your time, I could prove it.

AMBASSADOR: Really?

(ARNIE AND THE AMBASSADOR LEAVE THE ROOM FOR ONLY A MOMENT.)

AMBASSADOR: Security, toss Mr. Tiger and Mr. Knucklebreath from the building.

THE TIGER: What are you doing? What could that wombat possibly have told you that would cause you not to believe me?

AMBASSADOR: The truth.

• •

Then the scene ends. I was puzzled. I called Bill.

"Hey, Bill, did you get the revised script?"

"I did, Nick. I just finished reading it," he said.

"So you read the scene with The Tiger and the Felinia ambassador. What could Arnie the Wombat have said to the ambassador to disprove what The Tiger said?"

"That should be obvious, Nick," Bill said. "You can figure that out. I was glad though, to see the detective is a peacemaker in that scene."

"Why did you like that?"

"Because if Arnie is modeled after me, I'm glad to see him presented as a C.O.G."

"Like a cog in a machine?" I asked.

"No, those are just the first letters of a wonderful title," Bill said.

What did Arnie say to the Ambassador? And what is a C.O.G.? I don't think you'd be surprised to find out it has something to do with the Beatitudes of Jesus.

 **Turn to page 106 to find out!**

Chapter 9

The Case of the Preposterous Podcast

I was pretty popular on the first day of school. Before school and during the breaks all kinds of kids were coming up to me and saying, "Did you really meet Adam Lee Balmer?" or "Were you really on a movie set?"

And I could answer those questions. "Yes, I did." "Yes, I was."

But the next day, they were asking questions I couldn't answer. Cody Fargo asked, "Can you tell me the plot of the movie?"

Katie Bartlett asked, "What is Adam really like? What does he eat for lunch? How much money does he make?"

Alex Hampton asked, "Is the movie going to bomb?"

I couldn't answer a lot of questions people asked because I had signed a non-disclosure agreement. That meant I wasn't supposed to talk about anything that happened on the set or anything I read in the script until the movie was released.

So I wasn't so popular that day. In fact, Cody said, "I bet you never even saw the script."

Katie said, "I wonder if you really met Adam Lee Balmer."

And Alex said, "I bet you're just making up the whole thing. You probably spent the whole summer in your bedroom playing video games with your feet." *(I did spend a little time this summer playing video games with my feet. But just a little.)*

The next day was even worse. My friend Mike told me to look online for the newest podcast of *The Maple Dirt.* For the last year or so, someone (no one seemed to know who) started this podcast that spread gossip about our school.

Usually it was just stuff like "so and so" likes "so and so" or this guy got into a fight with that guy behind the cafeteria.

I tried to listen to the podcast at the school library, but it was blocked. Which probably was a good idea.

So after school, I went to Bill's office and asked if we

could use his computer to listen to it.

"I don't think that's a good idea, Nick," Bill said. "That's just a gossip site and nothing good comes from gossip."

"I know, but Mike said I should listen to it. He wouldn't tell me that unless he had a good reason."

So Bill went to his computer and played the podcast.

"This is the Shadow Reporter with the news you can use. Our first bit of news is about two popular students spied K-I-S-S-I-N-G under the old maple tree…"

I won't repeat any more of that story because it wasn't the one Mike had been talking about. But the next story was.

"Our newest connection to show biz, initials N. S., shared some dirt with me about the upcoming film with *Space Stuff* star Adam Lee Balmer. The film is about the adventures of a wombat detective. Because of that, N.S. tells me much of it is filmed during the day in woods around our town, showing the wombat with other native inhabitants like raccoons and squirrels.

"One of the reasons N.S. thinks the film will bomb is because of the disgusting scenes in the film of the wombat detective eating insects and even small rodents on top of his pizzas. N.S. said, 'No parent will allow their kids to see such gross stuff.' Sounds like a must skip film to me."

Bill muted the computer and looked at me. "I'm sorry, Nick, I know the answer to this question, but I need to ask it anyway. Did you say any of those things?'

"No, of course not. But I think I may know who…" Before I finished, the phone rang.

Bill answered it. "Good afternoon, Mr. Bowman. As a matter of fact, he's right here. Yes, you may speak to him."

I then had a very uncomfortable phone conversation with Detective Milo Bowman. He told me that the podcast of *The Maple Dirt* had gone viral; thousands of people had listened to it. A TV show, *Hollywood Currents*, was planning on broadcasting it.

And then he said that the studio lawyers were quite aware of who N.S. must be, and because I had signed the non-disclosure agreement, I could be sued for a whole lot of money. So much money that I would never go to college and my parents could lose our house.

I hung up the phone and for the first time in a while I felt like crying big time.

"Bill, I don't know what to do. I want to tell everyone

that the stuff on the podcast isn't true," I said. "But then I might have to say what I did see on the set and read in the script, and that would be breaking my agreement."

"Don't worry, Nick," Bill said. "We can work around the agreement. We can prove those things aren't true without revealing what's in the movie. And let me just say Nick, I'm impressed with how you've been willing to do what's right, whatever the cost the last few days. You've been living out one of the Beatitudes.

"Now you were going to say something before the phone rang. What was it?" he asked.

It seemed like a long time since before the phone call. Imagining your entire future being ruined makes time go very slowly.

"Oh, yeah. I was going to say I thought I recognized the voice on the podcast. I think it was Alex Hampton."

"Then let's pay Alex a visit," Bill said. "I think his podcast could use some real names rather than just initials."

I was surprised that Alex seemed to be expecting us.

"I thought that you might be coming to see me," Alex said. "Good to see you again, Bill."

"Alex, I'm in real trouble because of that podcast. You know none of it was true," I said.

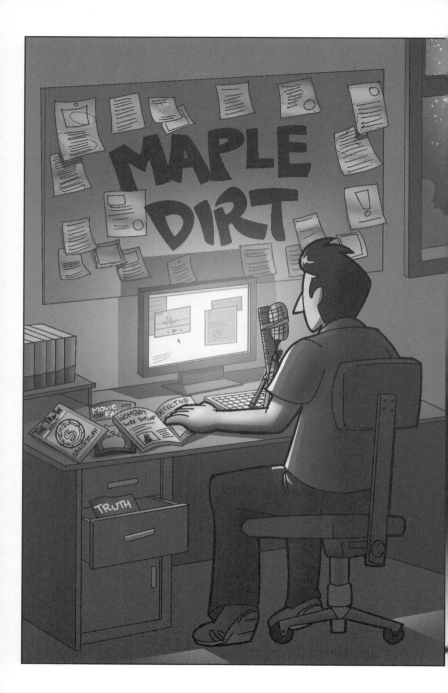

"Okay, Nick, then just let me interview you and you can tell what really happened on the set and what's in the script, and we can put this behind us," Alex said.

"That won't happen, Alex," Bill said. "We can prove the podcast was a lie without any mention of life on the set or the script. So you will let everyone know on your next and last podcast that you lied about Nick."

"And if I don't?" Alex said.

"Then everyone who you've gossiped about on your program will know who you are," Bill said.

How could Nick and Bill prove the podcast wasn't true without referring to the movie set or the script? What Beatitude had Nick been practicing (maybe without knowing it)?

 **Turn to page 108 to find out!**

Chapter 10

The Case of the Red Carpet Ruckus

Everyone in town was pretty excited when it was announced that *The Tiger Sleeps Tonight: The Adventures of Arnie the Wombat Detective* was going to have its world premiere right here.

Bill had told me it would take some months to edit the film, add special effects, add the music, etc. He said like anything worthwhile, it took time to do it right. The film finally had a release date, two weeks after the grand opening in our town.

But during those two weeks, another film was coming out. Republic International Pictures (R.I.P.) was going to release a film called *Alphonse the Bandicoot Investigator.*

I called Adam and asked him about this other film, and he told me his studio was concerned that R.I.P. might have made a film using ideas stolen from our film.

Adam invited us to ride with him in a limousine and walk down the red carpet at the premiere, but Bill had another idea. He thought there might be some security concerns at the theater so he volunteered us to help guard the theater.

I liked Adam's invitation better, but I said I would help Bill.

So Rudy, Adam's double, was going to walk down the red carpet with Adam. (Something exciting had happened the week before. Adam wanted Rudy to continue as his double on his TV show, and Rudy's dad got a job with the studio that makes *Space Stuff*. Rudy's whole family was moving to Hollywood.)

"So why do you think we need to worry about security for the film premiere?" I asked Bill.

"There's a so-called animal rights group, Wipe Out Wombat Oppression (W.O.W.O.), that's threatened to disrupt the screening," he said.

"I didn't know the filmmakers hurt wombats," I said.

"They didn't," Bill said. "The only wombat in the film is Arnie and he's just a computer animated figure. But I think

R.I.P. studios is using any means possible to attack our film and promote their rival film."

The night of the premiere, Bill and Milo Bowman had set up a plan for guarding the theater. The local police had officers watching the front of the theater (the south side of the building).

In addition to the cast of *Arnie,* many members of the cast of *Space Stuff* walked the Red Carpet too (including Martin Castillo who played the Captain, and Marv Martin who played the villain Slugtop.)

But there were three other entrances to the theater. Bill and I were to watch the west entrance, Milo Brown the north entrance and Milo's assistant Marvin Brown the east.

We were waiting outside the door when we heard a ruckus inside.

Opening the door, we saw about a dozen yelling and screaming protestors with signs.

"Nick! Quick!" Bill yelled. "Find a police officer and take him to the projection room!"

I ran to the front of the theater and found an officer. We ran up the stairs and found two members of W.O.W.O. trying to break into the projection room. The officer handcuffed them both and led them downstairs.

When I looked in the theater, everything had calmed down.

Apparently, when Bill told the protesters to settle down, they had to show him respect as a non-human mammal. They seemed puzzled as he asked them to please quiet down, form an orderly line and walk out the front door, where the police took care of them.

Mr. Gore went before the audience and said because of the disruption, the film would be delayed one hour. He offered everyone free popcorn and drinks while they waited.

In the meantime, Bill, Milo Bowman, Marvin and I met with the police.

I was shocked when Marvin said to the police, "I know who let in the protesters! I think it's the same person who has been working with Republic International Pictures all along.

"This person got the phony stunt man on the set; the same person bribed the gaffer and the caterer. It's the same person who let the protesters in tonight: Bill the Warthog!"

Milo said, "That makes a lot of sense. I always felt there had to be an inside person on the set who probably gave a

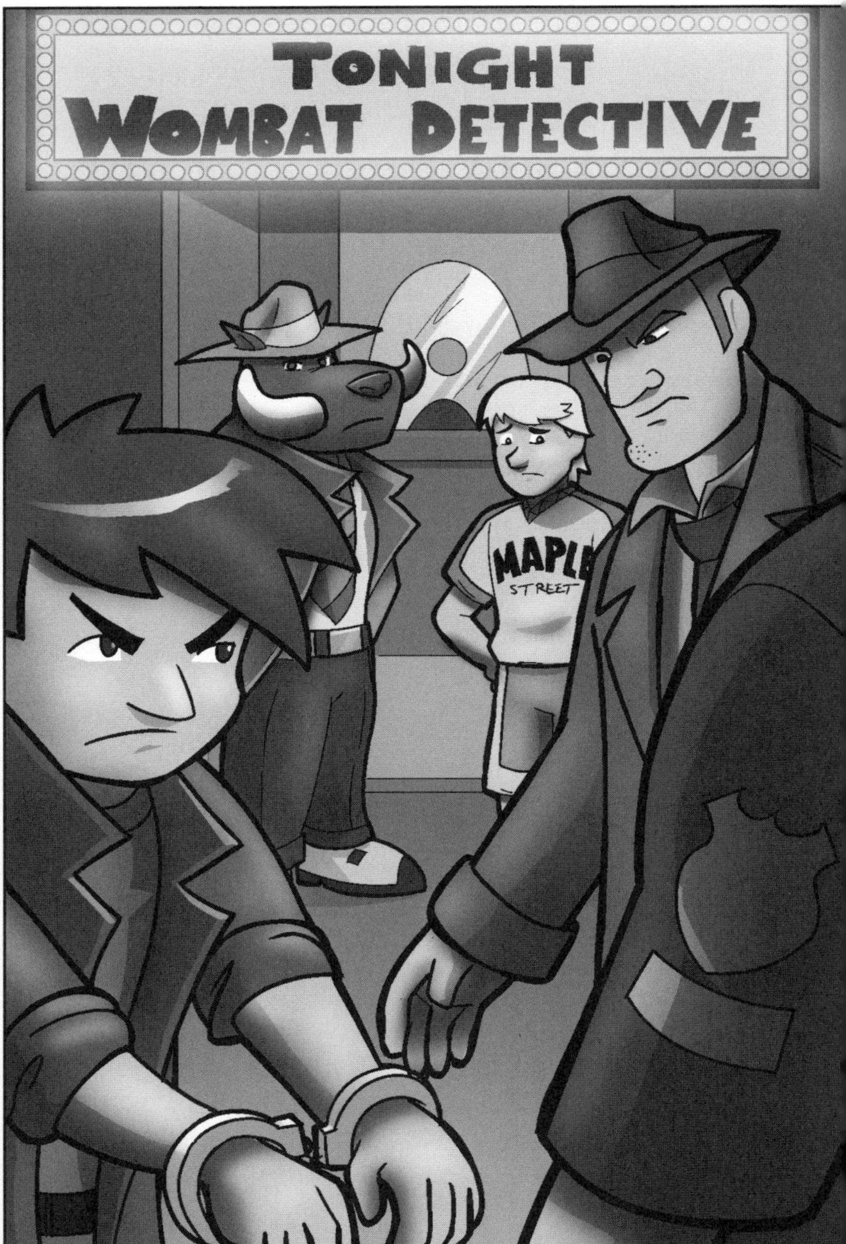
TONIGHT
WOMBAT DETECTIVE
MAPLE
STREET

script to R.I.P. That's how they were able to come out with a copycat film so quickly."

Officer Charlie Cruise said, "That is a very serious accusation, Marvin. You better have proof to back it up."

"Well, it might be his word against mine," Marvin said. "But I heard some noise and I looked around the corner of the building and saw Bill and Nick letting the protesters in through the door they were watching. You're not going to take the word of a warthog, are you?"

"Officer Cruise," Bill said, "may I speak with you privately?"

Bill whispered something to the officer. Officer Cruise then put handcuffs on Marvin Brown.

It was Milo's turn to be shocked. "Marvin, what is this about?"

"You barely paid me minimum wage, Milo!" Marvin yelled. "Republic Pictures was willing to pay me real money. And I could have got away with it too, if it wasn't for this warthog. And this kid. And the sloppy work of those protesters. And…"

Fortunately, the police hauled Marvin off so he wasn't able to go on with his excuses.

So we finally got to watch the picture.

I had to hush Bill, because he kept complaining about the "impossibilities" in the film.

But I thought it was pretty good, and so did the rest of the audience.

Afterward, I asked Bill if he wanted to go to the after-party. "Well, on the same night we've been accused of a crime, you want to go out and celebrate?" Bill asked. "Of course, it makes sense according to the Beatitudes. Let's go."

What did Bill tell Officer Cruise to convince him that Marvin was guilty?

And what does a party have to do with the Beatitudes?

☞ **Turn to page 110 to find out!**

The Case of the Rival Detective

Q: *What did Milo Bowman say that was wrong?*

A: Bill would probably have been quite happy to meet another detective. He would have loved to be able to talk about tricks of the trade and brands of fedoras.

But he was not very happy to be accused by Milo of offering a bribe.

Fortunately, he was able to prove Milo was lying with the very words of his accusation. Milo said that Nick and Bill had each offered "a bill." Not a Bill the Warthog kind of "bill," but a piece of paper money.

Milo said he was offered $50. But there are no two bills that add up to $50. There is a $50 bill. But no $25 bills. No $40 bill to go with a $10. No two bills add up to $50, which showed Milo was lying.

Q: *So, what are "Beatitudes?"*

A: Bill was referring to something Jesus taught. If you look in the Bible, in Matthew 5:3-12 and Luke 6:20-26, you can read about them.

Jesus taught that in the Kingdom of God, things are not always quite like you would expect. The poor are really rich. Those who are sad find true happiness.

Since things aren't always what they appear, it might end up that a warthog makes a better detective than Milo Bowman.

The Case of Seeing Double

Q: *How could Bill have proven that Rudy didn't copy the script with the copy machine?*

A: Rudy was suspected because the machine had been used to make extra copies.

But Bill said to Nick, "I have to hand it to you; you really put your foot in it this time." Bill could have examined the machine and found marks Nick would have made on the glass by putting his feet, hands, face, etc. on the glass of the machine.

If worse came to worse, he might have been able to get finger (or toe) prints and prove exactly who had been goofing off with the machine and made the extra copies.

Q: *What was Bill talking about when he talked about Milo Bowman's attitude toward the poor?*

A: Rudy and his family were obviously having a hard time. His parents needed work, so they didn't have much money for all the things other families have.

There are many people in the world who struggle to have enough money to get food, clothes and a place to live. Sometimes, people look down on others who are poor and think they are lazy or can't be trusted.

But one of the Beatitudes taught by Jesus is, "Blessed are you who are poor, for yours is the Kingdom of Heaven." God cares about people who are doing without. So if your family is going through a hard time with finances (money), you can ask God for help and know He cares.

And if you have enough (money, food, toys), you can know it will make God happy if you share with those who don't have what you have.

The Case of the Purple Tears

Q: *Why didn't Bill believe Eddie's tears?*

A: Bill didn't believe Eddie's tears, so he didn't believe his story. As he said, something didn't smell right. That's because he smelled onion.

He thought, perhaps, Eddie had eaten something that had onion like a sandwich or chili, but Eddie didn't admit to it.

The purple skin on Eddie's face came from an onion. An onion will bring tears to someone's eyes if they get their face close to it.

So sadly, the studio had to fire Eddie.

Q: *Why did Bill say that tears can be the beginning of blessing?*

A: Bill got a chance to talk to Eddie about the good thing about tears. In the Sermon on the Mount, Jesus taught, "Blessed are those who mourn (or who are sad)."

That sounds strange, because we don't think of being sad as a good thing at all. But it is good to be sad when we do something wrong. That shows we know it was wrong.

Jesus said God will comfort us when we are sad. That's true if we are sad because we have done something wrong, or because something bad has happened to us.

Oh, and as for Eddie, Bill talked to him and found out that someone had paid him to release the pictures on the Internet to make the movie look bad. Eddie had only heard from the person through text messages, so there was a lot more work for Bill to do.

Eddie apologized to Mr. Gore, this time with real tears. And there was some work for Eddie to do as well. Bill helped him get another job at the power company.

The Case of the Temporary Diamonds

Q: *Can you figure out how the diamonds were taken?*

A: The real puzzle in the script was how the cameras could film the diamond robber and yet not capture the robbery. The diamonds appeared to still be in the display case after the camera showed "The Tiger" leaving the room.

But Arnie the Wombat knew what had taken place (and so did Bill). Arnie showed he knew when he mentioned to the Tiger that diamonds are sometimes called "ice." That's why the Tiger pulled the lever — he knew he was caught.

Arnie had asked Stud if there was water on the floor, and Stud wondered how he knew. Arnie figured that the Tiger must have taken the diamonds and left something in their place.

The Tiger could have replaced the diamonds with glass fakes, but they would have remained (perhaps with finger prints of the thief). But Arnie knew that the real diamonds were replaced with fakes made of ice that melted away.

The motion-activated cameras would not record the slow process of ice melting.

Q: *What was Bill talking about when he said The Tiger should be more meek?*

A: In the Sermon on the Mount, Jesus said, "Blessed are the meek, for they shall inherit the earth."

Being "meek" is the opposite of thinking a lot of yourself (like the Tiger did).

Being "meek" doesn't mean you think of yourself as dirt. It just means you realize that like every other person on earth, you need God's help.

If you go to God and say, "God help me be the person you want me to be," He'll do that. He promises if we trust in Him, we can then know Him. There's nothing better.

The Case of the Peanut Dust

Q: *How did Bill know that Rodney was lying?*

A: Rodney said that he was a squirrel expert and then said he was going to portray an Australian squirrel.

Bill knew this wasn't true because though there are more than 200 types of squirrels in the world, none are in Australia, the home of the wombat.

Rodney admitted he had been hired by someone to put ground up peanuts in the salsa that went on Adam's omelet. He didn't know who had hired him. Someone called him and left him an envelope with money and the promise of more money later.

Q: *What did Bill mean by "hungering for what's right?"*

A: Again, back to the Beatitudes in the Sermon on the Mount. Jesus said, "Blessed are those that hunger and thirst for righteousness for they will be filled."

We all get hungry or thirsty at times and most of you who read this book have the resources to get food or water to meet that need.

That's a good thing. Our bodies let us know that food and water are needed. Jesus said it is an even better thing when we want to do what's right.

This is a great promise. If we want  to do what's right (obey our parents, be kind to others, tell the truth), then Jesus says God will help us do what's right. Now if you'll excuse me...this food talk has gotten me hungry. I'll be right back.

The Case of the Sloppy Stunt

Q: *How did Bill know that Ralph was guilty?*

A: Bill thought Ralph hadn't come to film the stunt, but he talked to the woman in charge of the clothes to be sure.

Ralph had come to the set wearing a green shirt. The scene was going to be filmed with a green screen, so with what Ralph was wearing, he would look like a head and arms floating on the screen.

Bill talked with Ethel Noggin, the wardrobe person, and found out the stunt person was not going to be given another shirt to wear. And Ralph should have known that.

Q: *What do the Beatitudes have to say about mercy?*

A: It's perhaps understandable that after his experience, Nick wasn't feeling very merciful. But in the Sermon on the Mount (Matthew 5:7), Jesus said, "Blessed are the merciful, for they shall be shown mercy."

We all have times when we do the wrong thing and get

ourselves in trouble and need mercy, like when Nick climbed up high on the movie set where he shouldn't have gone and put himself in danger.

He could have been in big trouble, but Bill helped him. We all look for mercy at times from our parents, teachers, even our friends. We need it from God most of all. And people who need mercy shouldn't be stingy about giving it out.

The Case of the Z Word

Q: *What did Ian have in his pocket that showed he was most likely to be innocent?*

A: Nick had wondered why Bill had Ian and Shane empty their pockets, but he learned the reason when he saw Ian take something out of his pocket. It was a pen.

Obviously, an autograph hunter wouldn't just have an autograph book, but also a pen for signing the book. So Ian did have some problems getting the spray paint off his clothes, but he did get lots of autographs, which he was very excited about.

And Adam was glad that he didn't have to use the bad word because he would feel bad about using it. Marvin obviously didn't feel bad about using that word and others that are worse.

It is important that we consider the books we read, music we listen to and movies and TV we watch. If we take in things that have bad words and violence and such, they will affect the way we think and feel.

But Jesus said, what comes out of us is even more important than what goes in. In Mark 7:15, Jesus said, it's not what goes into a person that makes them dirty, but what comes out of a person's heart that makes them unclean.

Q: *What did Bill mean when he said people who are pure in heart will see something great?*

A: The really good news is what Bill was talking about. He was referring to one of the Beatitudes again, "Blessed are the pure in heart, for they shall see God." As Bill said, that's better than seeing any movie or TV show or anything else.

[Editor's note: "Zarp" is only a bad word within this book.]

The Case of Fighting Like Cats and Dogs

Q: *What could Arnie the Wombat Detective have told the ambassador to show that The Tiger wasn't telling the truth?*

A: The Tiger said that because the people of Felinia wore red, the dogs of Muttoria were being trained to attack people who wore red.

Arnie just had to tell the ambassador a simple fact: dogs are colorblind.

Dogs don't see red or any other color, so the dogs of Muttoria could not possibly be trained to attack people wearing red.

The Tiger was trying to make the people of Muttoria and Felinia fight each other. There are plenty of people in the world who try to stir up fights. There are people who love to be able to call out at your school, "Fight! Fight! Fight!"

But Jesus in Matthew 5:9 said, "Blessed are the peacemakers." Happy are people who help people work together rather than fight.

Q: *What is a C.O.G.?*

A: Jesus says peacemakers will be called "Children of God." That's what Bill was talking about when he said, "C.O.G." A Child of God.

Our God is a God of Peace. You can be like Him.

Instead of fighting with your brothers and sisters, find ways to get along.

Find ways to make peace with your friends and with other kids at school.

And God will give you the best title in the world: His Child.

The Case of the Preposterous Podcast

Q: *How could Nick and Bill prove the podcast wasn't true without referring to the movie set or the script?*

A: Nick had to prove that he didn't spill the beans about the wombat movie on *The Maple Dirt* podcast, and he had to do it without talking about what had happened on the set or about things in the script. Bill told him there was a way to do that.

Previous leaks had made it public knowledge that the film was about a wombat detective. So Nick could prove the podcast wasn't true by using wombat facts: the film wouldn't show wombats as natives of the local woods because wombats are native to Australia. Even then, they probably wouldn't have filmed during the day because wombats are nocturnal animals.

Also, wombats are herbivores and don't eat insects or rodents (especially on pizza).

Q: *What did Bill mean when he said Nick was living out a Beatitude?*

A: Nick wasn't telling anyone about the movie set or script because he had signed an agreement and because it was the right thing to do.

In Matthew 5:10, Jesus said, "Blessed are those who are persecuted because of righteousness for theirs is the kingdom of heaven."

Sometimes when we do the right thing, like obeying our parents or teachers, other kids will tease us. But Jesus has promised us that we will always be better off if we do what is right.

The Case of the Red Carpet Ruckus

Q: *How was Bill able to convince Officer Cruise that Marvin wasn't telling the truth?*

A: It was a matter of location. Bill and Nick were on the west side of the building and Marvin was on the east side of the building. They were on opposite sides of the building. So he couldn't have "looked around the corner" and seen Bill.

And the film did do well.

As you may remember, it opened at No. 1 at the box office and got an Academy Award for Best Sound Editing.

It helped some that when Marvin told his whole story, lawyers were able to keep R.I.P. from opening their bandicoot film.

To show their thanks, the studio gave a big chunk of money to Bill, who gave it to Nick's church to start a kids' film production team. Nick suggested they make a film about a ferret detective, but the director of the program didn't see how there could be any spiritual message in such a film.

Q: *What do the Beatitudes have to do with parties?*

A: At the end of the Beatitudes, Jesus says when you are falsely accused, "Rejoice and be glad, because great is your reward in heaven."

Jesus taught us in the Beatitudes that even if we are poor, sad and picked on in this world, we still can find joy. Because God will be with us. The good news is the Kingdom of Heaven is coming. Other good news: it's already begun.

This isn't just a book or a movie. The Kingdom is real. And it's here.